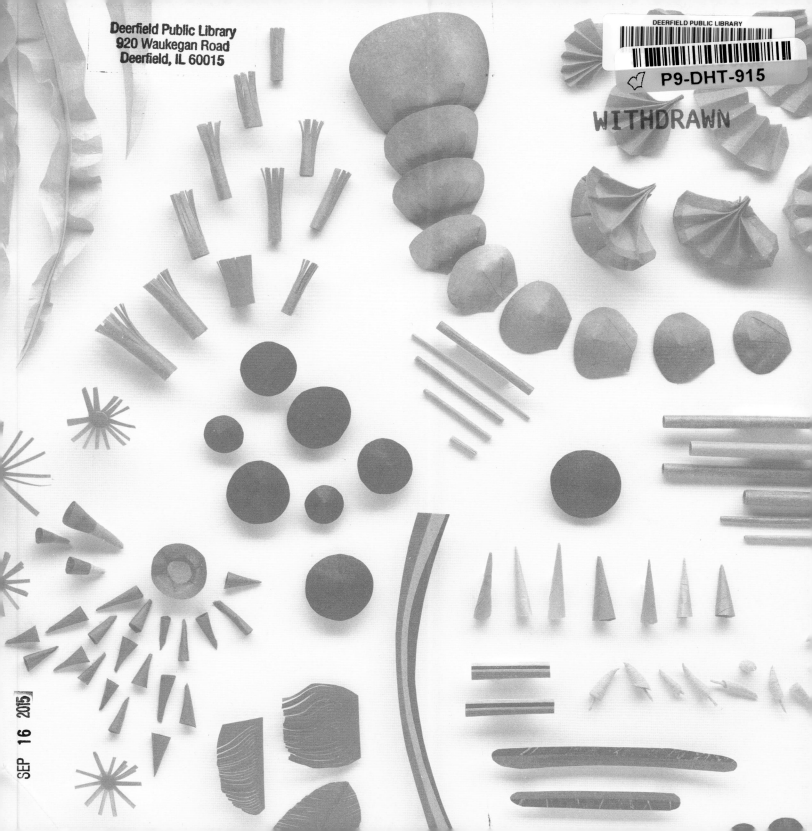

Groundwood Books / House of Anansi Press
110 Spadina Avenue, Suite 801, Toronto, Ontario M5V 2K4
or c/o Publishers Group West
1700 Fourth Street, Berkeley, CA 94710

We acknowledge for their financial support of our publishing program
the Canada Council for the Arts, the Government of Canada through
the Canada Book Fund (CBF) and the Ontario Arts Council.

Canada Council   Conseil des Arts
for the Arts   du Canada

ONTARIO ARTS COUNCIL
CONSEIL DES ARTS DE L'ONTARIO
an Ontario government agency
un organisme du gouvernement de l'Ontario

Library and Archives Canada Cataloguing in Publication
Young, Cybèle, author, illustrator
Some things I've lost / written and illustrated by Cybèle Young.
Issued in print and electronic formats.
ISBN 978-1-55498-339-1 (bound). — ISBN 978-1-55498-340-7 (pdf)
I. Title.
PS8647.O622S66 2015   jC813'.6   C2015-900032-7
C2015-900033-5

The sculptures in this book were made entirely from Japanese paper.
Design by Michael Solomon
Printed and bound in Malaysia

For Mary and Bill Corcoran

SOME THINGS I'VE LOST

CYBÈLE YOUNG

 GROUNDWOOD BOOKS   HOUSE OF ANANSI PRESS   TORONTO   BERKELEY

You can't find something,
something you've lost.
You've looked all around,
retraced your steps.
You've checked every possible place.

Where there's an end,
there's a beginning.

Things grow.
Things change.

Fig. 1
OBJECT: Roller skate
LAST SEEN: Basement — obstacle course

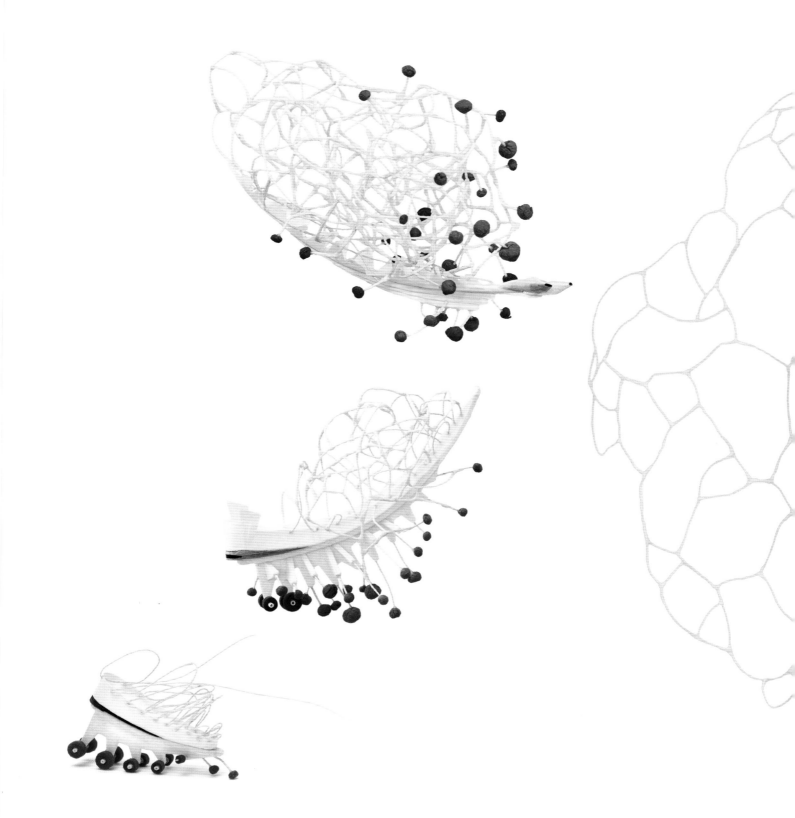

Fig. 2
OBJECT: Visor
LAST SEEN: Front lawn — lemonade stand

Fig. 3
OBJECT: Wristwatch
LAST SEEN: Kitchen — top drawer with
     the elastic bands

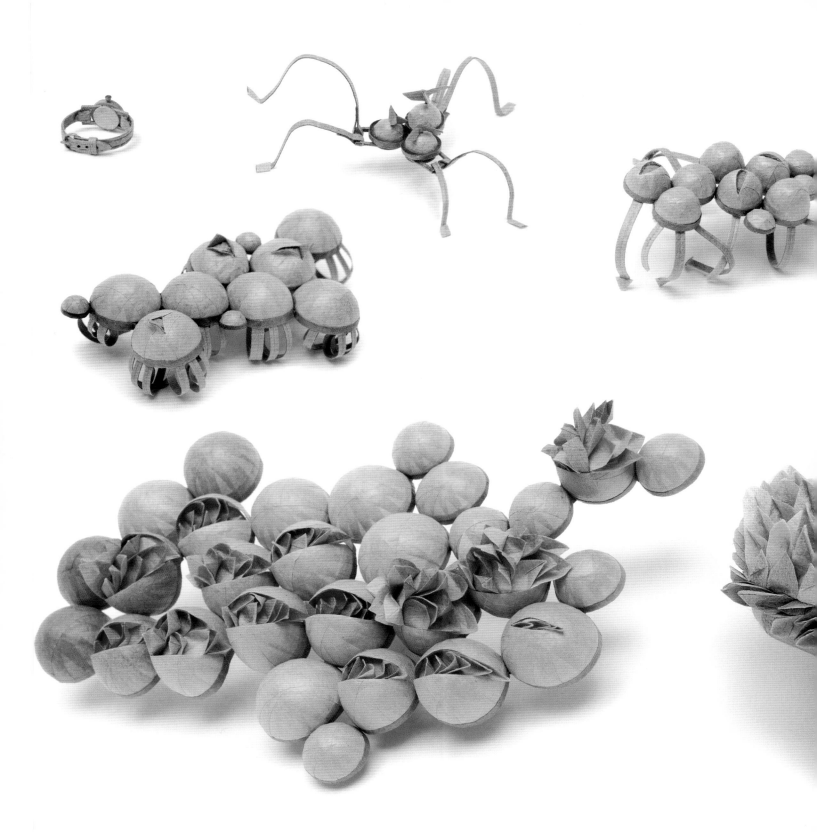

Fig. 4
OBJECT: Umbrella
LAST SEEN: Front porch with the others

Fig. 5
OBJECT: Dad's bag
LAST SEEN: Subway to work

Fig. 6
OBJECT: Binoculars
LAST SEEN: Backyard — meteor shower

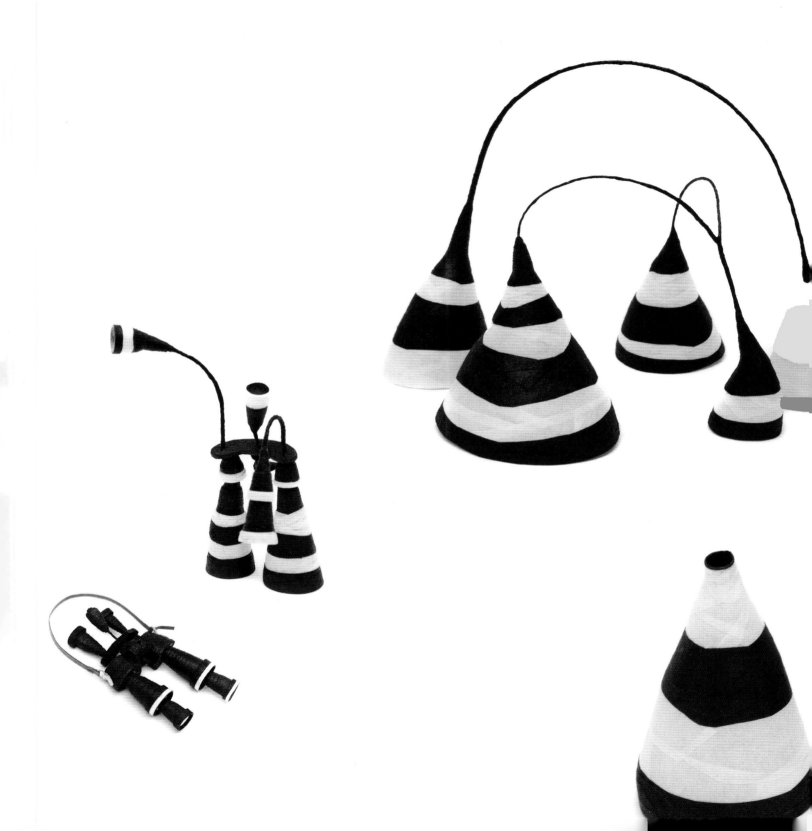

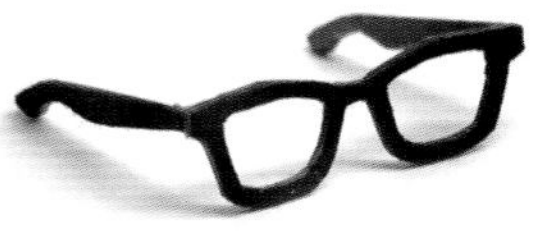

Fig. 7
OBJECT: Mom's glasses
LAST SEEN: On her head

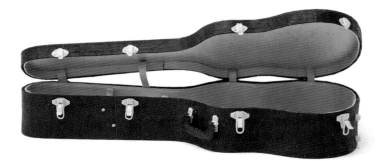

Fig. 8
OBJECT: Guitar case
LAST SEEN: Hillcrest Park —
     birthday party

Fig. 9
OBJECT: Change purse
LAST SEEN: Car ride home from the
    noodle house

Fig. 10
OBJECT: Sister's headphones
LAST SEEN: Could have been
anywhere, as usual

Fig. 11
OBJECT: Keys
LAST SEEN: Coat pocket — black or
brown one, not the red

Fig. 12
OBJECT: Lawn chair
LAST SEEN: Campfire —
     marshmallow roast

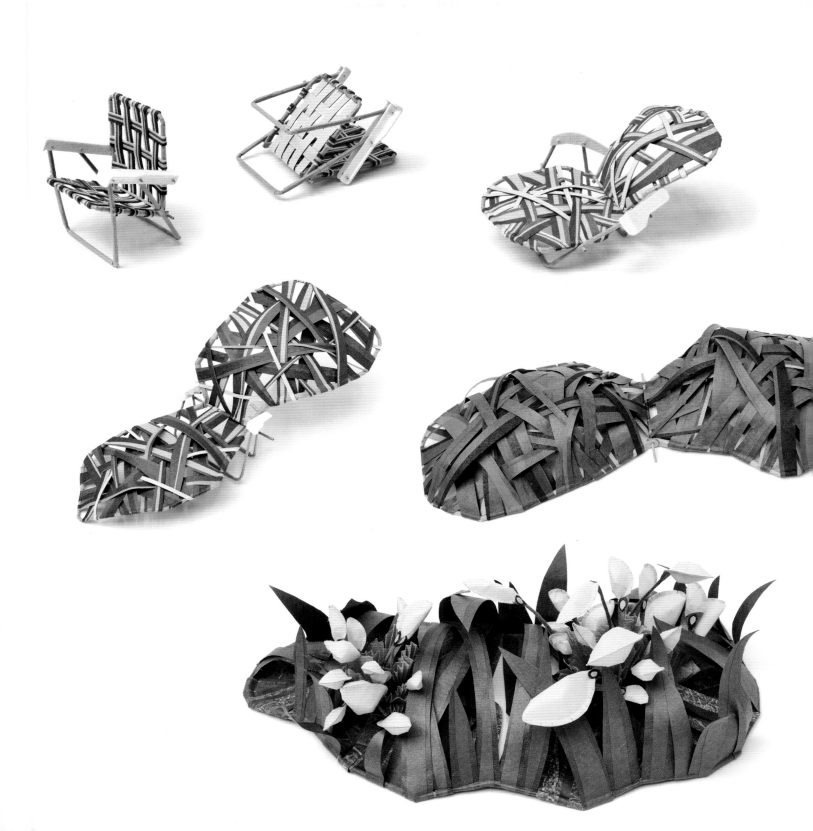

Anything is possible.

ACKNOWLEDGMENTS
My sincere thanks to Sheila, Michael and everyone at
Groundwood Books;
to Calder, Suzanne, ASV, Ezri, Leda and the studio crew;
and to the Toronto Arts Council, the Ontario Arts Council and
the Canada Council for the Arts for their ongoing support.
All photography by Dimitri Levanoff.